Numbers

Karen Bryant-Mole Edited by Jenny Tyler

Illustrated by Graham Round

About this book

This book is designed for an adult
and child to use together. As well as
providing all the guidance necessary to
ensure correct number formation, the
book aims to help your child enjoy
learning this new skill. There are hidden
numbers to discover and draw over,
and a variety of activities that will help
your child understand the mathematical
meaning of numbers as well as
giving invaluable practice
in pencil control.

GW00496998

Notes for parents

It is important to use this book when both you and your child are in the right mood to enjoy it. Do a little at a time and, if your child shows reluctance to carry on, stop and come back to it later. Remember that although some children find writing easy and enjoyable, for others it is a difficult skill to master.

Before starting to learn how to write numbers, your child needs to be able to control a pencil well. If they are still at the wild "scribble" drawing stage, it is too much to expect them to be able to manage the fine movements needed when writing complicated numbers. Tracing, dot-to-dot puzzles and colouring are all activities which help develop good pencil control. Another book in this series, *Ready for Writing*, is full of activities which help children develop the skills that lead towards number and letter writing.

How to hold the pencil

Always make sure that your child is holding the pencil correctly, as it is easy to develop bad writing habits with the wrong grip. Pencils should be held lightly between the thumb and the first two fingers, about 2cm (I in) from the point.

Number styles

As with writing letters of the alphabet, there is more than one style of number writing. No matter which style your child learns, or will learn at school, this book will still be helpful, as all styles use the same basic number formation.

Wherever possible, numbers should be made in one flowing movement and not in a series of disjointed shapes. An "8", for instance, should be made in a single stroke, starting with an "s" and then continuing back up with a reverse "s". An "8" should never be made by drawing one circle on top of another. The only single figure numbers that are made in more than one movement are "4" and "5". The sequence of numbers at the top of each page shows you how they should be drawn. It is important to learn to write numbers correctly from the start, as bad habits are very difficult to break.

Don't worry too much in the early stages about the reversal of numbers like 3 and 7. These are very common mistakes and ones which your child is likely to grow out of. The ones which are less noticeable but which they are less likely to grow out of are those concerned with formation rather than position, such as starting a 1 at the bottom instead of the top, or starting with the circular part of the 6 instead of the line. So, when your child copies a number, make sure that it not only looks right, but that it has been formed correctly too.

How the book is organized

The dot-to-dot activity on the first page of this book is designed to ensure that your child knows the correct sequence of numbers from I to I0. Each pair of pages then follows the same structure. The left-hand page shows your child how a particular number is formed. The following three lines give your child plenty of opportunity to practise writing that number. They can then enjoy looking for hidden numbers in the picture underneath and drawing over the dots. The opposite page helps your child to understand the mathematical meaning of the number through a variety of activities. The final page is a back-to-front dot-to-dot. Not only will your child have learnt about the sequence of numbers up to ten, but they can now try writing them too!

Join the dots

one

Cat and mouse are going to help you write your numbers.

- Join the dots to find some of the things you will need to do the activities in this book.

Cat and mouse's washing has blown off the line.

- Make I set of clothes that belong to cat by drawing a big loop around all the large clothes.

- Make I set of clothes that belong to mouse.

- Colour I sock in each set.

- Draw I button on cat's shorts.

- How many vests does mouse have?

two

The caterpillars are having a picnic too.

- Colour all the plates with 2 things orange.

- Colour all the plates with less than 2 things yellow.

- Colour all the plates with more than 2 things green.

- How many cups have 2 straws?

- Draw 2 straws in each of the other cups.

3 3 3 3 3 3 3 3 3

three

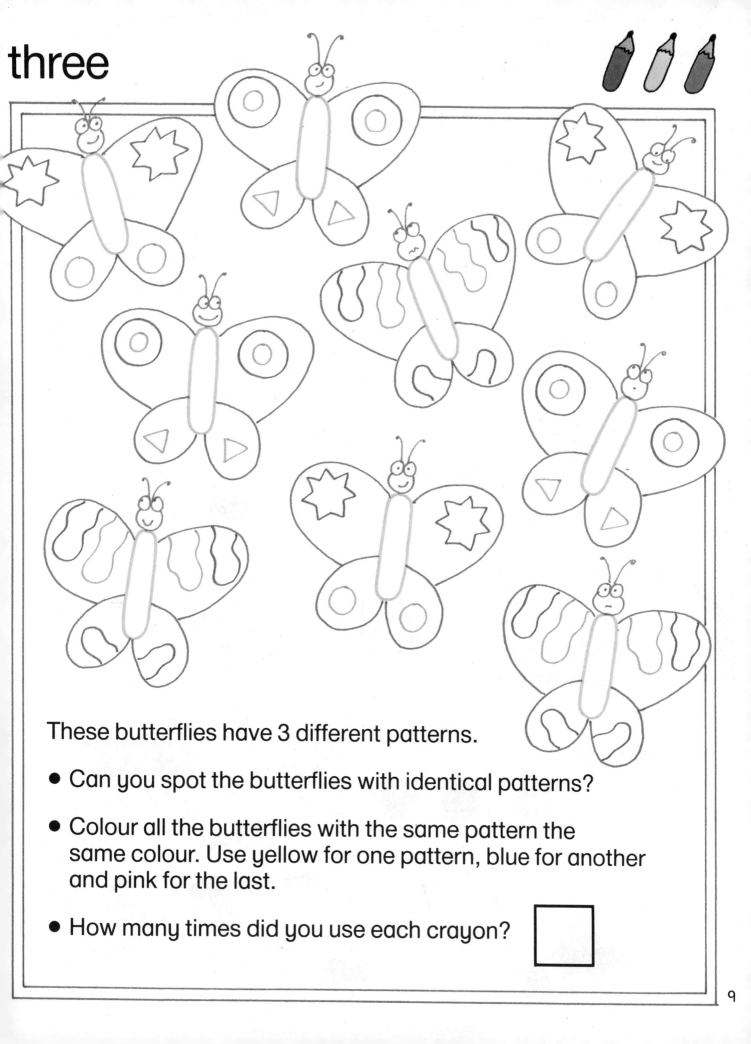

These butterflies have 3 different patterns.

- Can you spot the butterflies with identical patterns?

- Colour all the butterflies with the same pattern the same colour. Use yellow for one pattern, blue for another and pink for the last.

- How many times did you use each crayon?

4 4 4 4 4

4 4 4 4 4 4 4 4 4

4 4 4 4 4 4 4 4 4

four

- Count the number of sides on each kite.

- Who is holding the kite with 4 sides?
  Colour his hat red.

- How many bows has the kite with 3
  sides got on its tail?

- Add bows to each of the other kites so that each tail
  has 4 bows.

5 5 5 5 5

5 5 5 5 5 5 5 5 5

five

- How many balls is pig juggling with? ☐

- Is frog juggling with more balls or fewer balls?

- Look at the stars on their trousers.

- Colour all the stars that have 5 points blue.

- Colour all the stars that don't have 5 points yellow.

6 6 6 6 6 6 6 6 6

six

- Colour 6 of the presents around the tree.

- What do you think each present is?

- Cat and mouse have made paper chains.
  Cat used 6 loops in each of his chains.
  Colour cat's paper chains.

- Draw 6 decorations on the tree.

seven

Dog is painting his kennel.

• How many cans of paint is he using?

• Colour the paint cans using a different colour for each one.

• Use the same crayons to colour each plank in the side of the kennel a different colour.

• How many planks are there?

• Can you find 7 paint brushes hidden in the picture?

Cat and mouse are playing shops. They are using buttons for money.

- Colour 8 of the things in the shop.

- The spider should have 8 legs. Draw in the missing ones.

- How many things are there on the table?

- Which things cost 8 buttons?

q q q q q q

q q q q q q q q q q

q q q q q q q q q q

- Colour 9 bananas, 9 apples, 9 pears, 9 oranges and 9 pineapples.

- How many stripes are there on the stall's canopy?

- Draw 9 cherries in the tray marked

cherries

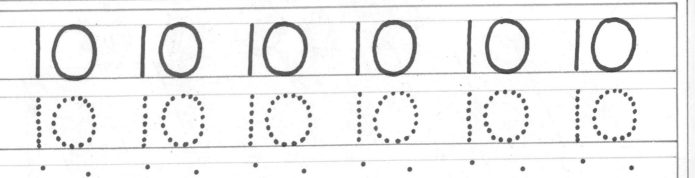

10   10   10   10   10   10   10

10   10   10   10   10   10   10

ten

- Use this outline of a head and body to draw your own space alien.

Give it:

1 mouth

2 noses

3 eyes

4 ears

5 legs and feet

6 arms and hands

7 fingers on each hand

8 tufts of hair

9 toes on each foot

10 spots on the tummy

Funny dot-to-dot

- Can you help cat and mouse with this back-to-front dot-to-dot puzzle?

- Instead of following the numbers and drawing the lines, you have to follow the lines and write in the numbers.

- Number 1 has been written in to start you off. Write a number next to each dot that you come to.